The Most Misplaced Angel

A Children's Story
by Clair A. Kozlowski

Scriptures Psalm 103:20 "Praise the Lord, you His angels, you mighty ones who do His bidding, who obey His Word." (NIV)

Copyright © 2024 Clair A. Kozlowski.

All rights reserved. No part of this book may be used or reproduced by any means, graphic, electronic, or mechanical, including photocopying, recording, taping or by any information storage retrieval system without the written permission of the author except in the case of brief quotations embodied in critical articles and reviews.

This is a work of fiction. All of the characters, names, incidents, organizations, and dialogue in this novel are either the products of the author's imagination or are used fictitiously.

WestBow Press books may be ordered through booksellers or by contacting:

WestBow Press
A Division of Thomas Nelson & Zondervan
1663 Liberty Drive
Bloomington, IN 47403
www.westbowpress.com
844-714-3454

Because of the dynamic nature of the Internet, any web addresses or links contained in this book may have changed since publication and may no longer be valid. The views expressed in this work are solely those of the author and do not necessarily reflect the views of the publisher, and the publisher hereby disclaims any responsibility for them.

Any people depicted in stock imagery provided by Getty Images are models, and such images are being used for illustrative purposes only.
Certain stock imagery © Getty Images.

Scripture taken from the Holy Bible, NEW INTERNATIONAL VERSION®. Copyright © 1973, 1978, 1984, 2011 by Biblica, Inc. All rights reserved worldwide. Used by permission. NEW INTERNATIONAL VERSION® and NIV® are registered trademarks of Biblica, Inc. Use of either trademark for the offering of goods or services requires the prior written consent of Biblica US, Inc.

ISBN: 979-8-3850-1825-3 (sc)
ISBN: 979-8-3850-1826-0 (e)

Library of Congress Control Number: 2024902342

Print information available on the last page.

WestBow Press rev. date: 9/4/2024

To my beautiful five grandchildren, Pierce, Brody, Logan, Elijah and Elyse. May they grow in their understanding of the great treasures of heaven given to men on earth.

The Most Misplaced Angel

On a clear and bright day, I think it was a Monday, all the beautiful angels gathered to do the word of the Lord in the heavenly realm. They were all very tall and very colorful. Many had their wings spread, and each one had a different sound making music in their fluttering wings. Flutter, flutter they went here and there, everywhere in the heavenly places, making music in their flutterings. Each one also had long, long walking in air legs. These long, long legs were a gift from the most wonderful God, whose throne room was at the highest point of heaven. Their very long legs caused them to fly even faster with their musical fluttering wings. Well… there was one angel who was kind of… different! Her name was Moreh. It means being sensitive and hard working. But no one knew her as Moreh. I believe they used to refer to her as… the Most Misplaced angel of all time. Among all of the angels who had the initial M on their robes, she was a little different! Her legs were shorter for some reason, than all the other angels. She had never received her walking-in-air legs, but she never complained. She most definitely had large wings, but she needed them to help her stand, not only to fly… When she tried to spread her wings to flutter away, she would attempt to keep up with the others with all of her might, and strive to be the fastest angel. But sometimes her sense of direction threw her for a loop, and she would get slightly confused going round and round through the dark clouds, which surrounded God's magnificent throne. Oh, oh, she would think "I don't want to get into another dilemma".

Moreh was a secret agent angel for the Most High God, meaning no other angel would be aware of the mission she would be assigned to. She had to be faithful and keep silent, go on her way, and be obedient to her task. She loved going to assist the humans on earth that always seemed to be needing help of some sort, even more than she did. Yes, Moreh felt she stood out for all the wrong reasons. She stood out because her hair wasn't exactly like the others. No matter what she did to it, she could not get it to look shiny, and flowing like she thought it should. Sometimes she felt like every day was a bad hair day. You see, her hair was short and of all things, was curly. What angel wanted curly hair? At least the humans couldn't detect her differences from all the other angels, because they could never see her. Sometimes she felt like the most disorganized angel OF ALL TIME. She thought, "if only I could get my walking-in-air legs." Then she would be able to make beautiful music with her fluttering wings. With her short legs she was never seen in the heavenly annual photos, because she was lost among all the other angels that stood so tall.

Trying to get through her day with more cheerful thoughts, the Most Misplaced angel decided to change a few things for the better. Maybe she was misplaced, she thought, perhaps those who refer to her as Misplaced were right. I think it's time to take some action, and even think of a new name, one associated with speed and strength, and being fearless! Yet, she could not decide which one to choose. It seemed every name beginning with the letter "M" had already been taken.

But, I will have to have it approved by the One who dwells in majesty in Heaven. The most misplaced angel remembered she already had a scheduled appointment with the magnificent God in Heaven. She would have to travel to an extremely high cloud to see Him in His throne room for her next assignment. He had told her not to fly anywhere, until she visited with Him first. She thought that was odd, because she usually never had to check in! She received her assignments and then she'd begin her journey. I love what I do, she thought, because as a secret agent angel I get to fly from heaven to distant lands all over the earth to check on God's beautiful children.

But this very day she had a book reserved that must be checked out at the Angel's Community Sky-brary. It was like the library that she saw people bring their children to and borrow new books to read and learn from. Well she thought, I will have just enough time to make a quick stop at the sky-brary to pick up a new copy of Angel hot breads and warm cakes. I do not want to miss out on some yummy new recipes for angel food, she thought, as she loved to bake and to entertain other angels.

Of course my new name would have to start with the letter M, as her initial "M" was already on every outfit she owned in her closet. Once that stop was out of the way, she decided to drop her new book off at her dwelling, and to put on a beautiful robe for her meeting with her wonderful God. She lived on a lovely skyway where all of the angels with the names beginning with "M" lived. Everytime she passed another angel making the most lovely music, she became more determined to become known by a brand new name.

There it was, her home on Starburst Highway in the sky. She had to pass a merger of Pinwheel and Sunflower Skyways. Now she was only seconds away from her front door. One more Spaceway to cross over, with Pegasus on the left, and Starburst the second right. In the front door she hurried and changed into her newest flowing robe, with the monogram "M" in gold on it.

With not a second to stop and look at her hair, as usual, she flew out her front door, getting excited as she thought of seeing Him on such a day as this one, wondering why He wanted to see her at all? Up, up she went to be in His very presence. Upon arrival, she rushed in. Standing on her short legs, and leaning on her wings, she lovingly bowed before Him. She knew she had to be very attentive, yet still find the time to tell Him about the whole truth of her dilemma.

Finally, she exclaimed to Him her reasons for wanting a new name. She just stood there, looking up with her round violet eyes, waiting with her fingers pressing against the palms of her hands… of course, the Most High looked with great concern, but was oh so happy to greet her. "You are known as The Most Misplaced Angel?" He said. "No, no, My sweet angel. Your name is Moreh, it is a beautiful name. That is what I wanted to see you about! You say you are known throughout My kingdom as the 'Most Misplaced Angel' but I am now giving you a new name. You will be called Moriah! One that will match the way I see you as. You have been a grand and noble secret agent angel, going on 3,973,254 angel assignments. Now you will be a musical angel. You will become known as the 'Most Musical Angel', not the most misplaced one. You were always right where you belonged! You thought you couldn't measure up to the other angels, and allowed them to distress you. But now your new mission will be to go to the 'land of vision,' which is in Israel." He continued, "You are called to go there frequently, with the other musical angels, and sing new songs of praise, to the glory of My Name…. Sweet angel Moriah, now that I have called you by your new name, no one will be able to call you another one." My new name rang in my ears so loudly, I was at a loss for words.

"From now on, you will have new responsibilities. Always remember what your true name means, see, I am giving you threads of silver, that will be woven through your golden monograms on each robe you wear. These silver threads will become invisible, but will enable you to have the ability to sing beautiful songs with the other angels in the 'land of vision'. You are, and always have been, a most treasured angel.

Oh, and one more thing Moriah, I also know about some disobedient angels that have been roaming about, where they ought not to go, calling out false names to My ministering angels." And so upon finding out how much He planned for her future, she was thrilled, and received God's new mission for her. Realizing no one else had that name, and that God had reserved it just for her, Moriah found herself glowing, and feeling confident, which caused her so much joy she couldn't help but stand quite tall. Actually... very tall, upon realizing she possessed her very own long, long walking-in-air legs, just like all the others she had tried so hard to keep up with.

She was filled with happiness, and soon she was able to spread her wings. They seemed to become more colorful than ever before. When she left, she felt herself thinking about her true name which had been a mystery to her. She couldn't imagine being named after God's very own "land of vision!" I should have never believed any spiteful name that was used against me. I listened for so long I began to believe silly nonsense.

Then came a wonderful surprise; as she started her flight to return home, she felt herself traveling swiftly through the clouds with very little effort. She was now appointed to go and sing wonderful new songs. "Wow, she exclaimed, I love to sing! "I'm so thankful for my secret name Moriah, now revealed to me." She swiftly flew back and forth. For the first time she heard the most beautiful music coming from her own fluttering wings. "How good it is to hear my own music and to love the sound of my new name." With her renewed assurance of where she was created to be in heaven, she shouted in great delight. "My name is Moriah, Moriah!!! I am loved, and highly treasured!" Off she flew, faster than ever before! To sing, of course!